Captain Crossbones
and the
Lost Treasure

illustrated by
NARINDER DHAMI ⚓ LUCY FLEMING

OXFORD
UNIVERSITY PRESS

Great Clarendon Street, Oxford, OX2 6DP,
United Kingdom

Oxford University Press is a department of the University of Oxford.
It furthers the University's objective of excellence in research, scholarship,
and education by publishing worldwide. Oxford is a registered trade mark of
Oxford University Press in the UK and in certain other countries

Text © Narinder Dhami 2017
Illustrations © Lucy Fleming 2017

The moral rights of the author have been asserted

First published in this edition 2019

British Library Cataloguing in Publication Data
Data available

978-0-19-276909-1

1 3 5 7 9 10 8 6 4 2

Paper used in the production of this book is a natural, recyclable product
made from wood grown in sustainable forests. The manufacturing process
conforms to the environmental regulations of the country of origin.

Printed in China

Helping your child to read

Before they start

- Talk about the back cover blurb. What might Captain Crossbones' treasure turn out to be?

- Look at the front cover. What kind of person is Captain Crossbones?

During reading

- Let your child read at their own pace, either silently or out loud.
- If necessary, help them to work out words they don't know by saying each sound out loud and then blending them to say the word, e.g. *a-ng-r-i-l-y, angrily.*
- Encourage your child to keep checking that the text makes sense and they understand what they are reading. Remind them to re-read to check the meaning if they're not sure.
- Give them lots of praise for good reading!

After reading

- Look at page 48 for some fun activities.

Chapter One

"My treasure is missing!" Captain Crossbones roared angrily. "Where, oh where, can it be?"

Captain Crossbones' real name was Emily, but she didn't like it when people called her that.

Captain Crossbones began to search her bedroom. It was one big mess. There were clothes and toys everywhere. Captain Crossbones looked in all the places she could think of, but her treasure had vanished. Vanished, just like that, into thin air!

"Someone's stolen my treasure," Captain Crossbones muttered, grabbing her cutlass. "Just wait till I find out who it is. I'll tie them to the ship's mast. I'll make them walk the plank. I'll feed them to the fishes!"

Captain Crossbones ran downstairs. Mum heard her and came out of the kitchen.

"Have you cleaned up your bedroom yet, Emily?" Mum asked.

"Shiver me timbers, Cook!" Captain Crossbones replied. "No, I haven't. My treasure's been stolen!"

"There'll be trouble if you don't tidy up that mess," Mum warned.

"Can we have fish and chips for dinner, Cook?" Captain Crossbones asked hopefully.

"Yes, but only if you tidy your bedroom!" Mum replied, and she went back into the kitchen.

"Oh no!" Captain Crossbones groaned. "I have to find my lost treasure quickly, so I have time to tidy my cabin before dinner. I need help. Where's my crew?"

Captain Crossbones whistled loudly. "Ahoy, Cut-throat Charlie!" she yelled.

Cut-throat Charlie trotted out of the living room, wagging his tail.

"We've got to find my lost treasure, Charlie," Captain Crossbones explained. "We'll need the help of Blood-thirsty Ben, the Terror of the Seven Seas!"

"Woof!" said Charlie.

Captain Crossbones knew Charlie was saying, "We'll find your treasure, Captain, even if we have to search for a hundred years!"

"Come on, my faithful friend," said Captain Crossbones. "We'll sail across the sea to Blood-thirsty Ben's ship next door and ask him to help."

Together, Captain Crossbones and Cut-throat Charlie hurried across the deck. But suddenly the bell rang.

"Who's this?" Captain Crossbones whispered. "Someone's trying to get on board our ship!"

"Woof!" said Charlie.

Captain Crossbones knew Charlie was saying, "We'll tie him up and feed him to the sharks!"

Chapter Two

"Ahoy there!" Captain Crossbones yelled. "Tell me who you are or I won't let you on board my ship. Are you friend or foe?"

"Friend!" shouted the person outside the door.

"It's our friend, Charlie," Captain Crossbones said. "It's Blood-thirsty Ben, the Terror of the Seven Seas."

"Woof," said Cut-throat Charlie happily.

"Ahoy, Blood-thirsty Ben!" said Captain Crossbones. "I need your help. A scurvy thief has stolen all my treasure!"

Blood-thirsty Ben looked shocked. "That's bad," he said.

"I have to find my missing treasure *and* tidy my cabin before dinner," Captain Crossbones told him. "Or Cook says I won't get any fish and chips."

"That's REALLY bad!" gasped Blood-thirsty Ben.

"We'll search this ship from top to bottom," Captain Crossbones said. "We'll ask everyone on board if they've stolen my treasure."

"We'll make them talk by tickling their toes," said Ben with a blood-thirsty grin.

"It's a deadly and dangerous mission," the captain said. "Are you with me?"

"Aye-aye, Captain!" Ben shouted, and Charlie barked loudly.

Captain Crossbones and her crew began looking for the lost treasure in the kitchen.

"You're getting under my feet," Mum said. "Mind the flour!"

"A scurvy thief has stolen my treasure, Cook," Captain Crossbones growled. "Was it you?"

"No, Emily, it wasn't," Mum replied. "Now go and play somewhere else!"

Dad was vacuuming the hall floor.

"Ahoy, ship's mate!" said Captain Crossbones. "The deck looks nice and clean. Keep up the good work!"

"Mind your feet, Emily," said Dad.

"A scurvy thief has stolen all my treasure," Captain Crossbones growled. "Was it you?"

"No, Emily, it wasn't," Dad replied. "Now go and play somewhere else!"

"Let's ask the ship's parrot," said
Captain Crossbones. "Ahoy, Poppy
the parrot!"

Poppy looked rather cross. "What do
you want, Emily?" she snapped. "Can't
you see I'm on the phone?"

"You're always talking, Poppy!"
Captain Crossbones growled. "Are you the
scurvy thief who stole my treasure?"

"No, Emily, I'm not," Poppy replied.
"Now go and play somewhere else!"

"The ship's cat might be the thief," Blood-thirsty Ben whispered.

"Grr!" Cut-throat Charlie growled at the sleeping cat.

"No, it wasn't the ship's cat," Captain Crossbones replied. "I think I know who stole my treasure!"

"Who?" Blood-thirsty Ben wanted to know. "Was it the ship's cook? Was it the ship's mate? Was it Poppy the ship's parrot?"

Captain Crossbones shook her head. "No, I don't think it was one of them," she said. "I think it was Oliver the Terrible. I bet *he* took my treasure!"

"Oliver the Terrible?" Ben gasped. "The most evil baddy in the whole world?" "Yes," Captain Crossbones replied.

Chapter Three

Captain Crossbones, Blood-thirsty Ben and Cut-throat Charlie raced to the captain's cabin to find her spyglass.

"Your cabin's a bit of a mess, Captain," said Ben, looking around.

"Never mind that now!" Captain Crossbones snapped. "We *must* find Oliver the Terrible and get my treasure back!"

Captain Crossbones put the spyglass to her eye and stared out across the sea. She could see Oliver the Terrible's fort not far away.

"I wonder if Oliver the Terrible is hiding there?" Captain Crossbones said.

"Maybe that's where he's taken your treasure!" replied Blood-thirsty Ben.

"Woof!" barked Cut-throat Charlie.

"We need a plan, Blood-thirsty Ben," said Captain Crossbones. "How am I going to get my treasure back from Oliver the Terrible?"

"WOOF!" Charlie barked at the top of his voice. "WOOF! WOOF! WOOF!"

Captain Crossbones and Blood-thirsty Ben turned around and saw that a note had been pushed under the cabin door.

"Good work, Cut-throat Charlie!" the captain whispered. "I think this might be one of Oliver the Terrible's tricks. Stand back while I take a look."

Captain Crossbones picked up the note and read it.

I HAVE KIDNAPPED ONE OF YOUR CREW.
ONE-EYED JACK IS A PRISONER IN MY FORT.
BRING ME TEN PIECES OF SILVER RIGHT AWAY, OR YOU'LL NEVER SEE ONE-EYED JACK AGAIN.
HA! HA! HA!
Signed, OLIVER THE TERRIBLE

"Oliver the Terrible has kidnapped One-Eyed Jack!" Captain Crossbones gasped. "And Oliver knows I can't pay ten pieces of silver because he stole my treasure! Didn't I tell you he was full of tricks?"

"Poor One-Eyed Jack," said Ben sadly. "What are we going to do now, Captain Crossbones?"

Chapter Four

"I'll tell you what we're going to do," Captain Crossbones said. "We're going to storm Oliver the Terrible's fort. We're going to free One-Eyed Jack and get my treasure back!"

"Woof!" Cut-throat Charlie barked excitedly.

"Let's go right away!" Blood-thirsty Ben shouted.

"Not so fast," said Captain Crossbones. "First we must arm ourselves."

"Are you ready, Blood-thirsty Ben?"
Captain Crossbones cried.

"Ready, Captain," Ben replied.

"Ready, Cut-throat Charlie?" asked
Captain Crossbones.

"Woof," said Charlie.

"Just remember that Oliver the
Terrible is *very* bad and *very* clever,"
Captain Crossbones said. "He'll try all
kinds of tricks, and we must be ready
for him!"

"Is it all clear?" whispered
Captain Crossbones.

"All clear, Captain," Blood-thirsty
Ben replied.

"Let's go," Captain Crossbones told
them. "But stay close to me and look
out for Oliver the Terrible. He may be
spying on us. He may even try to attack
us first!"

Captain Crossbones, Blood-thirsty
Ben and Cut-throat Charlie crept across
the deck. All the time, they kept a sharp
lookout for Oliver the Terrible.

Then suddenly a loud voice
shouted, "WAIT!"

"You made us jump, Cook!"
Captain Crossbones gasped. "We're
on the lookout for Oliver the Terrible.
Have you seen him?"

"No, I haven't seen your brother,
Emily," Mum replied. "He could be
outside in the tree house. It's you I want
to talk to. Have you cleaned up your
bedroom yet?"

"I can't do it right now, Cook,"
Captain Crossbones groaned. "I'm on
the trail of my stolen treasure."

"I'll check your room at six o'clock,
Emily," said Cook. "And if it's still a
mess, then no fish and chips for you!"

Captain Crossbones looked at the
ship's clock. It was half past five.

"Shiver me timbers!" Captain
Crossbones gasped. "There's no time
to waste."

Chapter Five

Captain Crossbones, Blood-thirsty Ben
and Cut-throat Charlie set off towards
the fort.

"Ssh, don't make a sound," the
captain said. "We're going to attack
Oliver the Terrible in his fort and take
him by surprise."

Soon the captain, Ben and Charlie were standing under the tree house. They could hear loud, crunchy noises coming from inside.

"What's Oliver the Terrible doing up there?" Blood-thirsty Ben whispered.

"I hope One-Eyed Jack is all right," Captain Crossbones said with a frown. "Let's go and rescue him!"

The captain, Ben and Charlie burst
into the fort.

"We've come to rescue our crewmate,
One-Eyed Jack!" Captain Crossbones
roared. "And to get my treasure back!"

Oliver the Terrible jumped to his feet
and dropped the big bag of crisps he
was eating.

"Never!" he shouted. "I'll never give
up One-Eyed Jack. He's my prisoner!"

Captain Crossbones and Blood-thirsty
Ben tried to grab Oliver the Terrible,
but he was big and strong. He got away
from them, and the three pirates began
to fight.

"Grr!" Cut-throat Charlie growled
at the cat. The cat arched her back and
hissed. Then she chased Charlie around
the fort.

"Let One-Eyed Jack go, or you'll
be sorry, Oliver the Terrible!" Captain
Crossbones snarled. "And I want my
treasure back too, you scurvy thief!"

"I didn't steal your treasure," Oliver
replied. "But I *do* have One-Eyed Jack,
and he's staying here until I get my ten
pieces of silver!"

"You go and look for my treasure, Ben," Captain Crossbones shouted. "Leave Oliver the Terrible to me."

"Aye-aye, Captain," Blood-thirsty Ben replied, and he ran off to search the fort for the captain's treasure.

Suddenly, Captain Crossbones spotted One-Eyed Jack. She ducked past Oliver the Terrible and ran to the other side of the fort. Then she grabbed One-Eyed Jack and gave him a big hug.

"Jack, I'm so glad you're safe," Captain Crossbones gasped. "Blood-thirsty Ben, did you find my treasure?"

"It's not here, Captain," Ben said. "I've looked everywhere."

"Stay away from my fort from now on!" Oliver the Terrible shouted. "Or next time I'll tie you up and tickle you till you can't speak! I'll spin you around until you're so dizzy, you can't see straight!"

"Well, we got One-Eyed Jack
back," said Captain Crossbones. "That's
good. But we didn't find my treasure.
That's bad."

"And we still don't know who stole
the treasure," Blood-thirsty Ben replied.

Captain Crossbones, Blood-thirsty
Ben, Cut-throat Charlie and One-Eyed
Jack hurried back to the pirate ship.

When they reached the deck, Captain
Crossbones looked at the ship's clock.

It was ten minutes to six.

"I've got to tidy my cabin now, before
Cook comes to check at six o'clock."
Captain Crossbones groaned. "Or there'll be
no fish and chips for dinner!"

Chapter Six

Captain Crossbones, Ben and Charlie rushed to the captain's cabin.

"Do you think we've got time to clean things up in ten minutes?" Captain Crossbones asked hopefully.

"No way," Blood-thirsty Ben said, sitting down on the bed. "It's much too messy!"

"Woof!" Cut-throat Charlie barked sadly.

"Ouch!" Ben gasped, jumping up again. "I just sat down on something hard and sharp."

"Did you hurt yourself, Ben?" asked Captain Crossbones. "What did you sit on?"

"I don't know," Ben said with a frown. "It's hidden under this pile of clothes."

Captain Crossbones and Ben pulled all the clothes off the bed to find out what he'd sat on.

"It's my missing treasure!" Captain Crossbones yelled happily. "Now I remember! I was going to count my gold and silver when I was in bed this morning. But I got up to take Charlie for a walk, and I forgot."

"So we got One-Eyed Jack back *and* we found my treasure," said Captain Crossbones. "But now we only have *five* minutes left to tidy my cabin before six o'clock."

"No fish and chips for you, Captain," Ben said sadly.

"Maybe it's not too late," Captain Crossbones said with a big smile. "I have an idea!"

"Emily, I'm coming to check your room," Mum called as she went upstairs. "If everything's clean and tidy, then I'll send your dad to buy fish and chips for dinner. But if your room's still a mess, then it's cheese on toast for you!"

"My cabin's really tidy, isn't it, Cook?" said Captain Crossbones proudly. "So can we have fish and chips, please?"

"Yes, we can," said Mum. "Would you like to stay for dinner, Ben?"

"Yes, please," Blood-thirsty Ben said eagerly.

"Woof," said Cut-throat Charlie.

"You can have fish and chips, too, Charlie!" said Mum.

"We found my lost treasure, we won our fight with Oliver the Terrible *and* we're having fish and chips for dinner," Captain Crossbones said happily. She hugged One-Eyed Jack. "It's great fun being a pirate!"

After reading activities

Quick quiz

See how fast you can answer these questions!
Look back at the story if you can't remember.

1 What is Captain Crossbones really called?

2 What does Captain Crossbones call her mum?

3 Why do Captain Crossbones and Blood-thirsty Ben want to tidy the bedroom?

Talk about it!

- How do you think Captain Crossbones and Blood-thirsty Ben manage to tidy the bedroom so quickly in the end?

- What do you do when you have to tidy your bedroom?

1) Emily; 2) Cook; 3) otherwise, there won't be fish and chips for dinner